Michael
Travels to
Nashville, Tennessee!

Michael Travels to Nashville, Tennessee!

Candace Ferdinand
Illustrated by Karine Makartichan

PALMETTO
PUBLISHING
Charleston, SC
www.PalmettoPublishing.com

Copyright © 2025 by Candace Ferdinand

Illustrated by Karine Makartichan

All rights reserved

No portion of this book may be reproduced, stored in a retrieval system, or transmitted in any form by any means—electronic, mechanical, photocopy, recording, or other—except for brief quotations in printed reviews, without prior permission of the author.

Hardcover ISBN: 9798822972070
Paperback ISBN: 9798822972087

Dedicated to my son Michael,
and all the autistic children in the world.
"You can do amazing things."

I love you.

Hi! I'm Michael, and I'm five years old.

I have mild autism, but I don't let that stop me from having fun.

In fact, I recently traveled to Nashville, Tennessee on an airplane!

It was my first time flying on an airplane, and gee, talk about being afraid. I was so afraid, and panicky at first, but then I started to calm down, as Mom gently laid her hand on my chest and softly said,

"There's nothing to be afraid of, Michael. You're okay. You're all right. Take a deep breath, and just relax."

That day, I overcame my fear of flying with the help of my toys, snacks, headphones, tablet, and my MOM!

Come on, turn the page, and let me tell you all about my fun adventures in Nashville, Tennessee!

Interesting Fact: Raleigh, North Carolina's RDU Airport offers nonstop flights to Nashville, Tennessee's BNA Airport with a flight time of less than two hours. This is pretty awesome for kiddos just like Michael who may need a quick flight for a vacation destination.

When I arrived in Nashville, Tennessee I was so hungry that all I could think about was food.

Luckily for me, my family was hungry too, and we quickly arrived at a mouth-watering and plentiful breakfast buffet.

Whoa! Strawberry pancakes! Blueberry pancakes! Plain glazed donuts! Chocolate glazed donuts! Blueberry donuts! You name it! Warm, soft, and flaky biscuits, as well as eggs, toast, and all of my favorite fruits: grapes, blueberries, apples, and bananas!

Food galore!

I was so excited that I jumped up and down with joy! I even rocked from side to side and hummed my favorite tunes while eating my scrumptious breakfast.

I was already liking Nashville, Tennessee, and enjoying my summer family vacation.

Interesting Fact: Nashville, Tennessee is known for its signature foods and dishes including hot chicken, Tennessee whiskey bourbon steak, barbecue, fried catfish, biscuits, fried pickles, and fudge pie.

After my tummy was full from all the yummy food I ate, I went on an incredibly cool riverboat ride.

It was amazing!

I saw lizards. No thanks.

I don't like bugs and reptiles.

I saw lots of beautiful trees and bushes along the river bend. The water was calm and peaceful, as the riverboat glided down the river.

I looked to my left and my right, taking in every view of the river.

The sky was perfect and blue, with just enough clouds for me to gaze up at, but not enough to hide the beaming sun. It was hot, and I was ready to go to the hotel room, relax, and play with my toys.

Interesting Fact: Nashville, Tennessee has three main rivers: the Cumberland, Stones, and Harpeth. The Cumberland River stretches 687 miles through the city and is Nashville's primary source of water.

The next day, I rode on a horse carousel five times!

It was awesome; my horse lifted me up and down and went around in circles.

"Whee, whee, whee," I happily said repeatedly.

I really enjoyed the carousel music too. I shook my head from side to side and tapped my feet to the sounds of circus music.

I was having a blast seeing all of the majestic colors: blues, yellows, whites, and pinks, and the twinkling lights that sparkled off of the horses.

I wanted to stay and ride on the carousel all day, but it was time for lunch.

Interesting Fact: The Fox Trot Carousel created by Red Grooms, a local Tennessee artist, operated from 1998 to 2003. The Fox Trot Carousel was unique, whimsical, and beautiful in its own way. Instead of a traditional carousel, the Tennessee Fox Trot Carousel featured 36 figures from Tennessee history. From President Andrew Jackson and the Everly Brothers, to the Goo-Goo Boy, these sculptures represented past times and historical events treasured by the artist and many others.

For lunch, I had a large slice of pepperoni pizza that I enjoyed cramming into my mouth.

The pizza was so good and flavorful with lots of cheese and just the right amount of tomato sauce and herbs-and not too spicy!

I also had a rich and creamy vanilla ice cream cone for dessert.

It was hard to put down!

This was truly a fun vacation so far!

I was surprised at how delighted I was in eating good food and dessert while experiencing the new scenery in Nashville, Tennessee.

I wasn't afraid!

Interesting Fact: Goo Goo Cluster is a chocolate candy dessert invented in Nashville, Tennessee in 1912. It is multi-layered with chocolate-covered candy bars, and if that's not enough, it boasts caramel, marshmallow nougat, and roasted peanuts in milk chocolate. DE-LI-CIOUS!

Then, I did something really COOL!!!

Later on that day, I got to play on a professional drum set in a real recording studio with gleaming lights, and instruments-all for me to make incredible noise and music with.

It was a good time.

I got to bang, play, hit, and beat with two drumsticks on a drum set with cymbals. What a super-fun experience.

I was happy and unconfined.

I could play as long and loud as I wanted without anyone telling me to STOP or to be QUIET.

I wasn't afraid. I wasn't nervous.

I wasn't worried about being in another city or another state; I was blissful just being a kid.

Interesting Fact: Nashvox Studios, a professional recording studio, in Nashville, Tennessee offers 60-minute private recording studio sessions. You'll have the time of your life playing various instruments and recording a song of your choice with your family and friends!

The following day, I got to run and play outside and touch the water in this humongous water fountain. It was so tall and huge!

Mommy told me to play and have fun, and I did just that.

I would touch the water with my hand, snatch my hand back really quickly out of the water, and then laugh profusely.

I would pretend that the water was chasing me. I would stop and then run fast all around the water fountain. Again, and again.

"*YOU* can't catch me! I'm too *FAST!*"

The water fountain and I had a blast.

Interesting Fact: Among Nashville's premier parks, Centennial Park is one of the most popular. It's in a prime location and provides entertainment for the community, featuring several festivals, fairs, and music series throughout the year.

Next, Mommy and Grandma took me to this cowboy retail store with boots, shoes, hats, and clothes EVERYWHERE!

No matter where I looked, there were cowboy boots, hats, belts, and clothes. I thought it was a bit much, but Mommy wanted me to try on some cowboy boots, clothes, and hats.

For some reason, Mom thought it would be fun to dress me up in cowboy attire, so I did what I do best: I begged for her phone so I could watch cartoon videos.

I figured her phone would help keep me entertained while she had her fun dressing me in these funny clothes.

But, what the heck!

I'm usually a good sport, so I just smiled and laughed.

Interesting Fact: Although Nashville is the capital of Tennessee and is known as "Music City" for country music and other music genres, the average Nashvillian does not walk around dressed in cowboy or cowgirl attire. Locals in Nashville, Tennessee typically wear casual clothing. It is rumored that if someone is dressed in cowboy attire, it is a dead giveaway that he or she is most likely a tourist.

Later, Daddy and Grandpa took me to a video arcade.

I'm not into playing video games just yet, but I sure do enjoy smashing down all of those buttons on the arcades to see them light up!

Oh, boy, what fun!

If you haven't figured me out yet, it doesn't take much for me to have fun. I can have fun all by myself, and that's the joy of it.

Having fun wherever you are, and whomever you're with or not with.

Just let loose and have FUN!

Interesting Fact: The Great Big Game Show is an adult amusement center in Nashville, Tennessee known for its realistic game show environment, featuring a televised game show, lights, music, and even a host! You're sure to have fun cheering on your family and friends!

As we neared the end of our summer family vacation, my family and I popped into a few gift shops.

My mommy always has to buy souvenirs and memorable gifts so we can treasure our family vacation memories.

I love souvenirs too as they help me remember the good times we've had while vacationing.

These are the two souvenirs that I picked out:

A Nashville teddy bear and a book about Nashville's Music City.

I can't wait to take these souvenirs home!

Interesting Fact: Made in TN gift shop in Nashville, Tennessee has just about everything you need for your souvenir and gift needs. From its categories Bath & Body, Candles, Kitchen & Dining, Baby & Toddler Apparel to Gift Baskets, Made in TN will be sure to supply you with whatever you're looking for!

So just like that,

I went, conquered, and had a wonderful time in Nashville, Tennessee with Mom, Dad, Grandma, and Grandpa!

You see, it's not so hard to overcome your fears.

Sure, it may seem hard and scary at first, but with a little help and support, you can achieve big goals, and be victorious over your fears and self-doubts.

Now that we know we can overcome our fears…guess what?

We can continue to overcome our fears!!!

And, that's the best part about it!

Interesting Fact: When you speak affirmations over your life and your child's life, those affirmations will most likely become reality. YOU are what YOU speak. YOU are what YOU believe YOURSELF to be. Even with a disability, say it and believe it, and soon you will see yourself as brave, strong, courageous, fun, and adventurous. It took the two months leading up to Michael's trip to encourage him by speaking affirmations into his life. Michael would constantly tell me "NO" and that he was afraid to fly on an airplane. He would repeatedly say that he was scared. But, with the constant encouragement of speaking affirmations, Michael began to believe that he was, in fact, BRAVE.

YOU too can be brave and travel on an airplane.

Happy Traveling!

www.ingramcontent.com/pod-product-compliance
Ingram Content Group UK Ltd.
Pitfield, Milton Keynes, MK11 3LW, UK
UKHW052025100225
454900UK00002B/6